D0132511

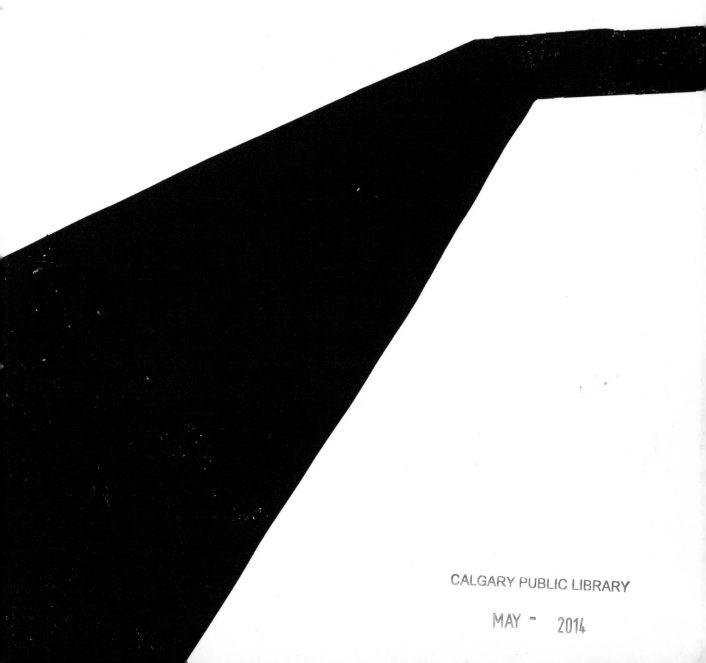

First published in English 2013 by order of the Tate Trustees
by Tate Publishing, a division of Tate Enterprises Ltd,
Millbank, London SW1P 4RG
www.tate.org.uk/publishing

First published in Portuguese as Para Onde Vamos Quando Desaparecemos?
© Planeta Tangerina, Isabel Minhós Martins and Madalena Matoso 2011
English language edition © Tate 2013

A catalogue record for this book is available from the British Library
ISBN 978-1-84976-160-4

Distributed in the United States and Canada by ABRAMS, New York
Library of Congress Control Number: 2013933771

Designed by Planeta Tangerina
Printed in Portugal by Printer Portuguesa

FSC
www.fsc.org
MIX
Paper from
responsible sources
FSC® C006423

# WHERE DO WE GO WHEN WE DISAPPEAR?

Isabel Minhós Martins
Madalena Matoso

Tate Publishing

Most of the time
we don't go
very far ...
We are just
around the corner.

Lying hidden,
with our eyes wide open,
waiting to be found.

If we disappear and nobody notices,
then we don't actually disappear.
Because for someone to disappear,
they have to be missed.


It always takes two
for someone to disappear.

(One that stays
and one that goes.)

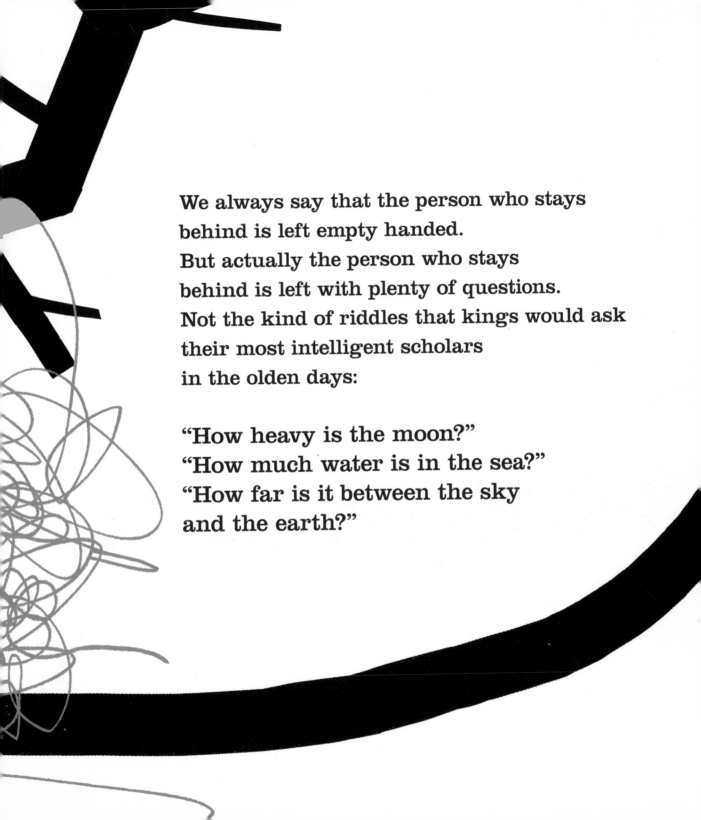

We always say that the person who stays
behind is left empty handed.
But actually the person who stays
behind is left with plenty of questions.
Not the kind of riddles that kings would ask
their most intelligent scholars
in the olden days:

"How heavy is the moon?"
"How much water is in the sea?"
"How far is it between the sky
and the earth?"

Usually the questions that are left behind
are far more difficult ...
After all, if you think about it,
scientists have now answered
nearly all of those questions.

But there are some questions they can't answer.
Spoken aloud in an empty room they
echo on forever:

"Where has she gone?"
"Will we ever see each other again?"

Fortunately
(or maybe unfortunately)
it's not just people
who disappear.
The same thing happens
to everything
in this world.

Sunshine,
clouds,
leaves
and even birthdays
are always
starting and ending,
appearing and disappearing.

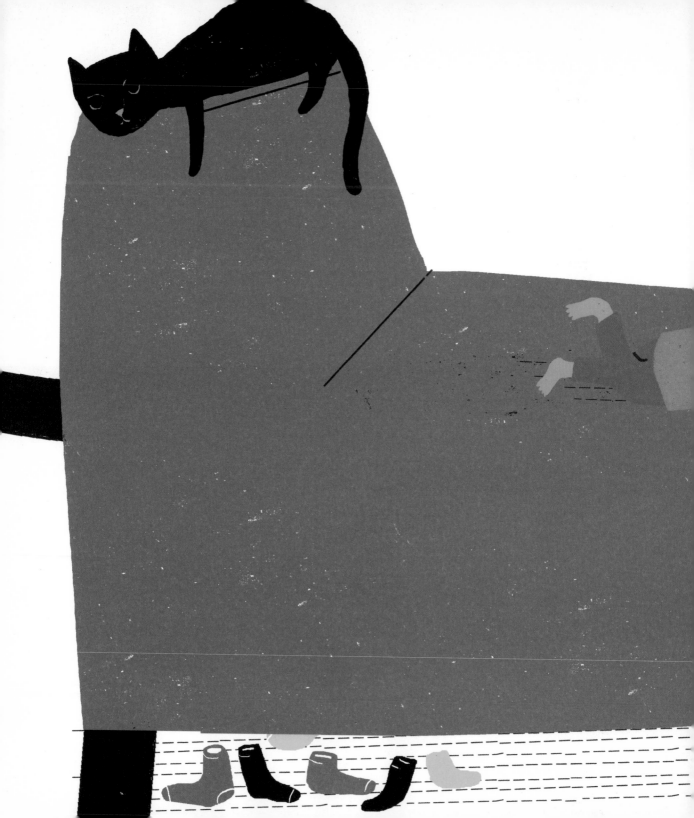

# Socks, for example. Where do they go when they disappear?

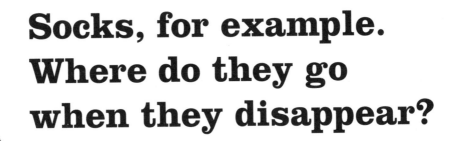

They might go to the dark world under the bed or far away down the back of the sofa. But quite often they disappear completely. If one day we find them again, we might discover they've been to amazing places!

# And what about puddles?

Once they've changed
into clouds, all puddles
go to heaven.

(Even the naughty puddles
that splashed us as we walked by.)

# And where do clouds go?

Clouds, sooner or later,
come back down to earth
as raindrops.
They come and go constantly
but we can sense they are still
with us from their shadows …

Boo! That means there
are ghost clouds on earth!

# And the sun?

The sun doesn't go anywhere … but we do.
We spin around on the earth and come back
messy and half asleep.

We say without thinking, "Oh look, the sun is rising".
But to the sun it's us that disappears and then rises again.

# And snow?

As soon as it arrives
the snow starts crying,
upset that it's about to disappear.
"What a pity, what a pity, what a pity ..."
It goes on for hours.

The poor thing doesn't realise
that the more it cries,
the quicker it disappears.

And noise, where does it go
when it disappears?

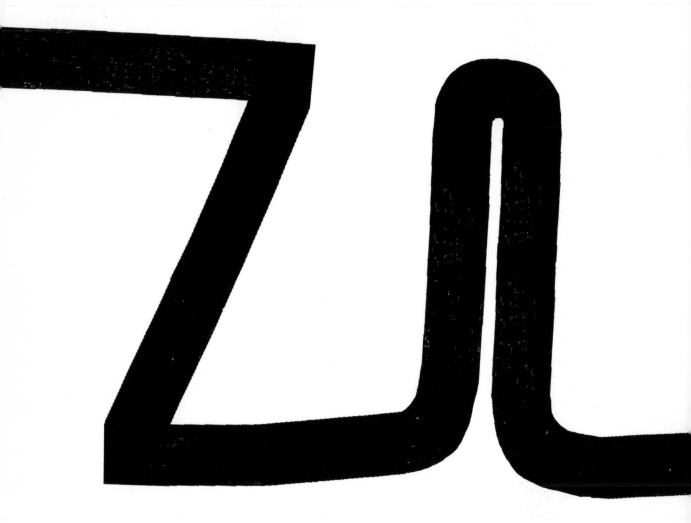

It stays buzzing in the air for a while
and then eventually falls silent.
But wherever children are running and playing
it immediately reappears.
There are certain places
noise will never disappear from.

# And where does everyone go at night-time?

Some people go home to sleep.
Others go out to dance.
Others do a little dancing in their sleep.

It's better than nothing …

# Nothing lasts forever.

Even something
as solid as a rock
will disappear one day.

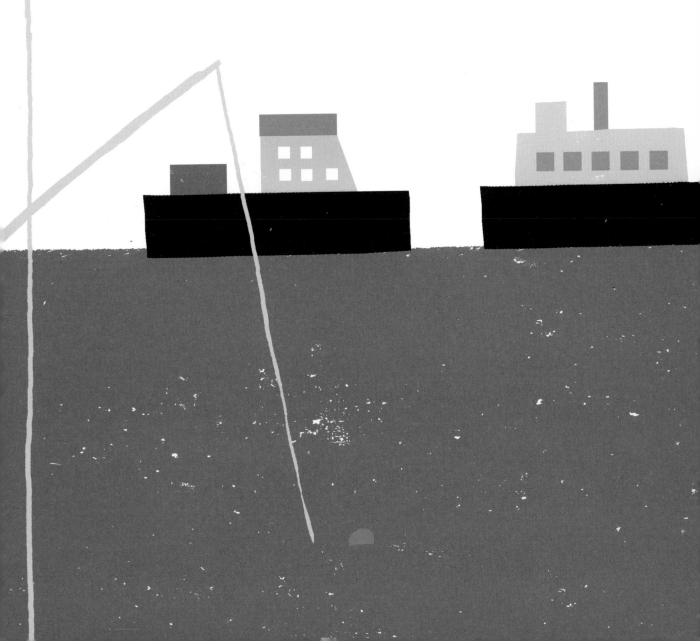

Rocks and cliffs
and stones take a long
time to disappear.

The wind tells them over and over:
"You cannot stay there forever ..."
The rain comes, waves come,
singing the same song over and over
as they ebb and flow until gradually
the rocks begin to crumble,
eventually turning into sand.

# And does
# the sand disappear as well?

(Every day beaches lose some of their sand to the tides.)

Sand disappears into the sea and travels
for miles and miles through the ocean.
Then, the next day, it comes back
as a different beach.
"The beach is as good as new!"
we scream with joy.

But we forget that when a beach changes shape,
it's because another beach has lost some of its sand.

Everyone says something different about where we go when we disappear. But if we look around us we'll discover even more ideas about what might happen.

Endless
possibilities.

We can go to amazing places (like socks).
We can go to heaven (like puddles).
We can travel through the ocean (like sand).
We can reappear (like noise).
We can stay exactly where we are (like the sun).

We can go to sleep or out dancing.
Or dance while we sleep.

# Better than nothing ...

Nothing is too empty a place to go.
And besides, if we all go there,
it will cease to be nothing in no time.
(We can't do that to it.)